Stock and Rocket

Published in 2024
First published in the UK by Stock and Rocket
An imprint of Igloo Books Ltd
Cottage Farm, NN6 0BJ, UK
Owned by Bonnier Books
Sveavägen 56, Stockholm, Sweden
www.igloobooks.com

0224 004
4 6 8 10 9 7 5 3
ISBN 978-1-78905-859-8

Written by Gemma Barder
Illustrated by Ela Jarzabek

Cover designed by Bethany Dowling
Interiors designed by Katie Messenger
Edited by Natalia Boileau

Printed and manufactured in China

This book belongs to:

....

Stock and Rocket

Gemma's Special Surprise

Gemma was the friendliest giraffe you could ever wish to meet.
She was always kind and polite, she gave everyone big giraffe smiles
each day, and, more than anything, she loved to help her friends.

Gemma would stretch up to the highest branch to reach the tastiest leaves for Zoe.

She gave Lenny a ride on her back when he was too tired to walk.

She even helped to untangle Emma's trunk.

Gemma's friends wanted to surprise her with an extra-special gift to say thank you for all her help, but they just didn't know what to get that would be special enough.

"I know!" said Zoe.
"Let's make a pie from tasty leaves."
But without Gemma's help,
no one could reach the best leaves
at the top of the tree.

Emma had another idea.
**"How about we make her
a beautiful flower bouquet?"**
So, she gathered the prettiest
flowers from all over the jungle.

But the flowers made Emma
sneeze and with one mighty
"A-A-CHOO!"
the entire bouquet
was blown away.

Just when the animals were about to give up hope of finding a special gift, Lenny jumped to his feet. **"I've got it!"** he said. **"Gemma helps us all the time. Maybe we should spend the day helping her?"**

The animals treated Gemma like she was the queen of the jungle.

Lenny brushed her mane...

... then Zoe polished her hooves...

... and Emma gave her a
relaxing neck massage.

"Helping is fun!" said the animals. Gemma smiled.
"And that's exactly why I love helping all of you," she said,
with a gigantic giraffe smile on her face.

Pepper to the Rescue

Pepper the puppy wanted to be just like his Uncle Rover,
a famous tracking dog who lived in the deepest jungles.

Although Pepper practised tracking
every day, he could never imagine
being as good as Rover.

One afternoon, while Pepper was tracking the scent of a
scurrying squirrel, his mum told him some very exciting news.

"Rover is coming to stay," she said. Pepper jumped for joy.
"I'll have to practise my tracking skills twice as hard now!"

The day of Rover's visit finally arrived. Pepper watched eagerly as Rover showed him his impressive compass collar. **"The most important thing a good tracking dog needs,"** said Rover, **"is his nose."**

"A-A-CHOO!"

Suddenly, Rover let out a big sneeze.

That afternoon, Pepper and Rover roamed through the forest, splashed through puddles and dug in the undergrowth. But poor Rover kept sneezing.

"Are you poorly?" asked Pepper, looking concerned.
"Of course not!" replied his uncle. "Us tracking dogs don't get sick."

The next morning, Pepper bounded downstairs for
more fun with Rover, but he was nowhere to be seen.

"Rover went tracking early this morning,"
said Pepper's mum. "He's been gone quite some time."

Pepper decided to look for Rover using the tracking skills his uncle had taught him. In the garden, Pepper found Rover's lost compass in the grass.

Next, Pepper sniffed and sniffed and soon discovered a scent trail.

Following his nose, he found a trail of paw prints, too!

The paw prints led Pepper to the forest.
Suddenly, he spotted Rover looking very lost.

"Thank goodness, Pepper!"
said Rover. "I think I might have
a cold after all. I lost my compass
and couldn't sniff my way home."

Back home, Rover gave Pepper his very own compass. **"It's used by the best tracker dogs and after today, that includes you,"** he said, proudly. Pepper gave him a big cuddle. **"I have the best teacher, ever,"** he said, smiling.